Here are some other Redfeather Books you will enjoy

The Curse of the Trouble Dolls
by Dian Curtis Regan

Max Malone the Magnificent
by Charlotte Herman

A Moon in Your Lunch Box
by Michael Spooner

The Peppermint Race
by Dian Curtis Regan

The Riddle Streak
by Susan Beth Pfeffer

Sable
by Karen Hesse

Sara Kate Saves the World
by Susan Beth Pfeffer

Sara Kate, Superkid
by Susan Beth Pfeffer

Snakes Are Nothing to Sneeze At
by Gabrielle Charbonnet

Tutu Much Ballet
by Gabrielle Charbonnet

Twin Surprises
by Susan Beth Pfeffer

Twin Troubles
by Susan Beth Pfeffer

Weird Wolf
by Margery Cuyler

Available in paperback

Susan Rowan Masters

illustrated by Beata Szpura

Libby Bloom

A Redfeather Book

Henry Holt and Company • *New York*

Henry Holt and Company, Inc.
Publishers since 1866
115 West 18th Street
New York, New York 10011
Henry Holt is a registered
trademark of Henry Holt and Company, Inc.
Published in Canada by Fitzhenry & Whiteside Ltd.,
195 Allstate Parkway, Markham, Ontario L3R 4T8.
Library of Congress Cataloging-in-Publication Data
Masters, Susan Rowan.
Libby Bloom / Susan Rowan Masters; illustrated by Beata Szpura.
p.   cm.—(A Redfeather Book)
Summary: When Libby, a fourth-grader who envies the
accomplishments of her older sister, begins tuba lessons
with a perceptive band teacher, she discovers that she has
hidden talents of her own.
[1. Self-confidence—Fiction.   2. Schools—Fiction.   3. Tuba—
Fiction.   4. Sisters—Fiction.]   I. Szpura, Beata, ill.
II. Title.   III. Series: Redfeather books.
PZ7.M423946Li   1995   [Fic]—dc20   94-43898

ISBN 0-8050-3374-2
First Edition—1995
Printed in Mexico
on acid-free paper. ∞
10   9   8   7   6   5   4   3   2

To my mother, and in memory of my father

Special thanks to my editor, Donna Bray,
and to the members of my writers' workshop
                                    —S. R. M.

To my niece, Paulina Maida, the toughest gal
in all of Great Bend, who one day may become
an artist . . . or a nurse!

                                    —B. S.

Contents

Libby Bloom

Good-bye, Mr. Walinsky

IT'S FUNNY how a dumb thing like a burp could change a person's life, Libby later decided. All it took was one measly burp to set off a whole chain of events.

If that burp hadn't happened when it did, and if Mr. Cheney hadn't been looking for someone to join band, and if a bunch of other disasters hadn't happened along the way, she would have stayed forever regular ol' Libby Bloom, still singing her heart out in chorus. Instead, she ended up becoming a local celebrity.

It all started fourth period, exactly one week before the Lincoln School chorus was to put on the fall concert. As usual, Mr. Walinsky was waving his arms in Libby's direction.

"Not so loud . . . softer . . . *softer!*" Mr. Walinsky shouted above the strains of "O Beautiful This Land."

But the notes were too high, and unless Libby pushed the words out extra hard, her voice sagged. Of course, she didn't want Mr. Walinsky to accuse her of singing off-key on purpose again. So over everyone else she sang, "Above rolling hills and mighty mountains the starry skies . . ."

Charlotte Whippo, who sat directly in front of Libby, stuck her fingers in her ears and scrunched up her tiny nose.

Libby pretended not to notice as she strained out the words, "O beautiful, O beautiful this land . . ."

As everyone paused for Charlotte to sing her solo, Libby burped. She tried covering it up with her hand, but that didn't help much. "Oh," she said in a small voice, "excuse me." She felt her face turning red.

Except for her friend Ralph Corbet, all the boys were rolling in their chairs, guffawing.

Above the laughter rose Charlotte's voice. "She did it on purpose."

"I did n—"

"She's going to *ruin* our fall concert, Mr. Walinsky."

"But I—"

"Just because *I* was chosen to sing the—"

"Read my lips!" yelled Libby, shaking her music book at Charlotte. "I don't give a rat's ear." The book flew out of her hand. It sailed past Charlotte and hit Mr. Walinsky.

Ten million freckles on Mr. Walinsky's balding head suddenly turned flaming red. "Go to the office," he demanded, pointing at the door.

While Mr. Walinsky turned his attention to the chorus, Libby slid out the door. At the principal's office, she slouched into one of four wooden chairs lining the wall. The secretary looked up from her computer. "What are you here for?"

"Mr. Walinsky sent me."

The phone rang. Before picking it up, the secretary said, "Mrs. Krauss is out right now, so you'll have to sit there quietly till she returns."

Since twenty minutes of chorus remained, Libby had plenty of time to sit and think. If only she could be more like her older sister. Noel's bedroom dresser was lined with trophies she'd won at swim meets and certificates she'd gotten for Outstanding Choral Performer in grades four, five, and six. Why couldn't it have been Noel instead of Libby who was a little afraid of the deep end and terrified of the diving board? "A natural athlete," "a breathtaking singer," people often called Noel. Nobody ever called Libby either of those.

Mrs. Krauss never did show up, but Mr. Walinsky did. At the end of the period he came to the office and motioned Libby over to him. "Have you considered joining band?" He let out a long sigh. "Mr. Cheney could use another student. And we're not so far into the school year that you couldn't switch."

As part of the music program all the fourth and fifth graders had to join either band or chorus. Libby chose chorus. It was her chance to show everyone what she could do.

"I hope you will seriously think it over," continued Mr. Walinsky before he turned to leave.

At the end of the day while everyone was getting ready to go home, Libby thought over Mr. Walinsky's words. Was her singing that awful? Of course, Noel thought it was. But then Noel thought everything Libby did was awful. She remembered asking her dad once, but he had only smiled and said something about singing being a celebration of life, and that everyone should sing. He didn't say if her singing was good or not.

The dismissal bell rang then and Libby, hurrying to join her class in line, grabbed her book bag. If she had known someone was coming around the corner at the exact moment she was swinging her bag over her shoulder, she would have waited a second longer to let that person pass. Unfortunately, her book bag and the principal collided. Mrs. Krauss ended up with her glasses perched crookedly on the tip of her nose.

"I-I'm sorry," gasped Libby. Before Mrs. Krauss could adjust her glasses, Libby disappeared around the corner and melted into the line waiting by the staircase.

Ralph Corbet's class got to the school exit ahead of Libby's. "Wait up for me," called Libby, waving at him.

"That's a heck of a right arm you've got," said Ralph, grinning as he fell in step beside Libby.

"I didn't mean to throw my music book. Anyway," added Libby, "Walinsky won't have Libby Bloom to kick around anymore." She kicked a stone and watched it skitter across a lawn. "I'm switching to band."

"This is a joke, right?"

Libby shook her head.

"I hear Mr. Cheney can be one strict teacher," said Ralph. "Besides, who wants to be stuck in the Dungeon for a whole period?" The band practiced down in the basement next to the boiler room. There used to be a real band room, but two years ago it was turned into a kindergarten.

"I can't believe you dropped chorus."

"Well . . ." began Libby, lowering her voice. She looked around to make sure no one was within earshot. "Mr. Walinsky didn't give me much choice."

"Never fear," Ralph whispered back. "That bit of information will never pass from these lips." Then he pretended to lock up his mouth and throw away the key.

"Thanks."

Ten minutes later Libby ran up the front porch steps into her house. Dropping her books on the side table, she hung up her jacket and hat and went into the kitchen. The door to the refrigerator, which faced her, was wide open.

"You'd better save me a piece of cheesecake, Noel." Even the thought of cheesecake topped with cherries couldn't keep her mind off the horrible day she had. "Stupid chorus," Libby muttered under her breath.

Just then her mother's head popped up from behind the refrigerator door, and Libby's heart took a flying leap.

Mrs. Bloom took a round container out of the freezer. "The cheesecake is gone." Her mother's words, Libby noticed, were laced with guilt.

"*All* gone?"

"How about strawberry yogurt to make amends?" Mrs. Bloom said, dishing some out.

Libby flopped down on a chair and dove her spoon into the bowl of yogurt. Then, as matter-of-factly as she could, Libby said, "Mr. Cheney is looking for another student to join band. I've decided to switch from chorus. It's no big deal," she quickly added.

"Are you sure this won't be any problem with Mr. Walinsky?"

Libby, shaking her head, put her empty bowl in the sink and dashed upstairs to her room. Across the hall Noel was practicing for her starring role in the upcoming junior-high musical. Libby closed her door, shutting out her sister's voice. The last thing she needed was to be reminded of her own failure.

Libby picked up a paperback mystery and sprawled out on the bed. Around the edges of the back cover were lacy patterns she had doodled during English class yesterday while Mrs. Petrush was going on and on about contractions. On the inside covers were drawings of a cartoon character she had created called Stretch McKinsy. Stretch wore the same kind of hat as Libby, and got into the same kind of trouble she did, which made Libby feel better. Burping in chorus didn't seem as embarrassing in a cartoon. In fact, it was pretty funny.

Libby was on chapter six when Mrs. Bloom called

everyone to supper. Libby put down her book and headed for the stairs. But she didn't get far before Noel came bounding out of her room and blocked the way.

"I can't believe my own sister acted like a hog today," said Noel.

Libby tried to explain. "It was just a teensy, tiny bur—"

"Bobbie's sister Michele told her about it and she told me. It's totally embarrassing to be related to you."

"Huh! You're a million, billion, zillion times more—"

"Honestly, Libby, when are you *ever* going to grow up?" Noel spun around and started downstairs.

If Noel thought being related was embarrassing, how would she feel if she had to *be* Libby Bloom, the most embarrassing girl in fourth grade?

2

Hello, Mr. Cheney

THE NEXT MORNING Libby went straight downstairs to the Dungeon. Opening the door, she peered inside. It was empty.

She was about to leave when she heard, "Come in." Mr. Cheney was sticking his head through the open doorway of his tiny office in the far corner. Libby could see Mike Macy sitting inside. "I'll be with you in a few minutes. Take a seat." Mr. Cheney ducked his head back into the office and closed the door.

The muffled sounds of Mr. Cheney's deep voice began filling the room. Libby caught snatches; something about being on time from now on for practice or . . . Or what? Libby wondered as she strained to listen. She had a feeling that it had to be something terrible because suddenly the room got quiet.

The door to the office burst open and Mike trudged out. Mr. Cheney motioned for Libby to come in.

As Libby slid past, she noticed Mr. Cheney had to stoop under the doorframe when he went back inside his office.

"You must be Libby Bloom. Mr. Walinsky told me you might be in to see me about joining band." Mr. Cheney thought a moment before adding, "Don't you have an older sister? Noel, right? A very talented student, too."

Libby blushed then, but Mr. Cheney didn't seem to notice.

"I can't believe what good timing this is. My tuba player moved away right after the beginning of school, and now you appear at my door." He leaned back and folded his arms.

"Tuba?" The word stuck in her throat.

"Unfortunately, the tuba is the only instrument available right now. Are you still interested?"

Libby looked past the open door into the Dungeon. How could she possibly miss seeing the tuba? It loomed like Godzilla from the back of the room. Libby shuddered. But did she have any choice? she thought before nodding.

"Glad to have you aboard," said Mr. Cheney. "Now, let's see what we can work out for your lessons." He placed a pair of reading glasses halfway down his nose and looked at a paper on his desk. "Who is your teacher?"

"Mrs. Petrush."

"In that case I'm scheduling your lessons for fourth period Thursdays and Fridays. Next we need to discuss what time you'll be practicing here after school."

"After school?" Libby repeated to make sure she heard correctly.

"It's either after school here," Mr. Cheney said, "or lug the tuba home for practice." He peered over his glasses and grinned. Smoothing back his thick mustache, Mr. Cheney looked at a weekly time chart. His pen was poised over the blank three o'clock Monday slot. "How's Monday?"

It stinks, Libby wanted to say. Instead she nodded.

"All the lessons in the world won't do any good unless *you* take the time to practice," reminded Mr. Cheney. "That means making the effort to get here at three sharp." He sounded like a general barking out orders.

Somehow Libby managed to go from horrible Mr. Walinsky to even more horrible Mr. Cheney.

As Libby was leaving, Mr. Cheney abruptly stood and followed her out the door. "You know, Libby," he said, locking the door behind him, "the tuba can be fun once you get the hang of it."

Libby made a face but made sure Mr. Cheney didn't notice.

"What instrument did you finally settle on?" Mrs. Bloom asked Libby that night during supper.

"Tuba," Libby answered in a quiet voice.

"Tuba? Did you say *tuba*?" asked Noel, looking up from her plate.

Nodding, Libby impaled two carrots on her plate.

"What? Burping isn't enough? Now you want to go around honking on a tuba?"

"Tubas don't *honk*!" Libby protested. "They . . ." What did they sound like? She had no idea.

"I don't think you need much musical talent to play one anyway," continued Noel. "So it's perfect for someone with a tin ear, like you."

"Noel!" scolded Mrs. Bloom. "That's enough."

Mr. Bloom winked at Libby. "Don't pay attention to Noel," he told her. "You do what you want."

But it wasn't *at all* what Libby wanted. What she wanted was to sing as well as Noel and have people tell her how great she was. A horrible thought crossed her mind: What if tubas did honk? That was all she needed. . . .

Friday morning Libby told Ralph about her meeting with Mr. Cheney. "What if he had asked you to play something bigger?" asked Ralph.

"Like what?"

Ralph opened the front door to Lincoln School and went inside. "Pipe organ." Then he laughed like it was the funniest joke he'd ever told.

"Go ahead, make fun." Libby trooped down the hall and into the classroom opposite Ralph's.

Libby spent the morning drawing her trademark along the border of her notebook papers. It was a cartoon figure she called Stretch McKinsy who, except for being short, resembled Libby herself.

"Libby," called Mrs. Petrush from her desk, where she was correcting math papers. "Don't you have your music lesson now?"

Libby glanced up at the clock over the front blackboard. It was six minutes after eleven. Oh, no. She was already a minute late.

Libby found Mr. Cheney in the Dungeon. But not pacing the floor as she expected. Instead, he was leaning against the far wall upside down on his head. His shirtsleeves were rolled up, and his necktie hung over his face. Libby's mouth dropped open as she watched Mr. Cheney flip back to his feet.

"Seeing the world from a different angle gives one a whole new outlook on things. And besides," added Mr. Cheney, brushing off his hands, "it's good for the circulation."

Libby followed Mr. Cheney over to the tuba. Even though she had never actually tried standing on her head, Libby decided that with all the blood rushing to her brain, her head would hurt. "Looks like a good way to get a headache."

Mr. Cheney's deep laughter bounced off the concrete walls. "The secret is getting used to it. Take this tuba," he began while Libby settled into the metal folding chair beside him. "Looks pretty imposing until you get used to playing it."

Libby had an idea what imposing meant as she stared at the huge mouthpiece aimed in her direction.

"What we have here is the double-B-flat bass tuba. Maybe it looks overwhelming to you now, but you'll get acquainted with it soon enough."

Who is he kidding? Libby thought as she listened to Mr. Cheney explain how to blow through the mouth-

piece. When Libby tried it herself, all she got was a low crackly sound. At least it wasn't a honk.

"No, no. *Purse* your lips together, like this, and buzz them." Mr Cheney puckered up like a goldfish.

Libby tried again. *BRROOOM.* A deep rumble echoed off the pocked walls. It faded away, leaving only the sound of knocking and rattling from the boiler room across the hall.

Mr. Cheney furrowed his brow. "That happens every time the boiler starts up." When it was quiet again, he showed Libby where to put her fingers for the notes B-flat and C.

Libby struggled over the first two pages in her lesson book, trying to remember which valves to push. She also had to buzz just enough. If she didn't, the pitch would come out wrong and she would have to start over again until she got it exactly right.

Once it took eight tries before Mr. Cheney was satisfied. Her lips were starting to get numb and tingly, and she was getting lightheaded from all the blowing. Chorus was never, ever this horrible.

Just when she thought she would burst if she had to blow one more note, Mr. Cheney said with a toothy grin, "Play it again, Sam." Then laughing, he added in his normal voice, "Only kidding. We're done for now,

Libby. Thought you might like to hear my famous Humphrey Bogart impression, though."

"Oh," said Libby, relieved that the lesson was finally over. Maybe Mr. Walinsky kicked her out of chorus, but at least he didn't do weird things like stand on his head and impersonate people she had never heard of.

"Humphrey Bogart and Ingrid Bergman starred in a movie called *Casablanca* way back in 1942," continued Mr. Cheney. "It's become a big classic." Then using his Humphrey Bogart voice again, he said, "I've always been intrigued with Bogart's old movies." He flashed another toothy grin at her.

"Intrigued?" Libby wondered aloud.

"In the context I used the word, it means to be curious or interested in."

Mr. Cheney took off the mouthpiece and handed it to Libby. "You need to practice more on this. Take it home and work on it. Okay?"

All during practice Libby was intrigued—she really liked that word—with the black instrument cases lining the opposite wall. As she was getting up she asked, "Can you play all those, too?" and nodded in their direction.

"Well enough to teach beginning students. But if

you mean well enough to perform, then I have to say just the flute."

Big Cheney and a flute? Scratching her head, Libby wandered out of the Dungeon into the darkened hall-way. The boiler made one more clank and grew silent. *Creepy,* Libby thought as she fled up the staircase.

3

"Help Our Students Fail"

"I'M GETTING a pair of gray sweats just like Coach's," Ralph told Libby on Monday morning.

Last Friday, Mrs. Krauss announced over the PA that October 25 was Teacher Recognition Day. To celebrate, all the students were invited to dress up as the teacher they most admired. A lot of the boys chose Coach Dunn, while many of the girls settled on Ms. Humphries, the new creative-writing teacher.

"What about you, Libby?"

She shrugged. "Who cares?" Maybe if there was someone really special this year, she wouldn't have thought it was a dumb idea. Of course, if Mrs. Krauss had asked them to pick the teacher they admired *least*, Mr. Walinsky would win hands down.

Libby reached into her book bag. She took out the tuba mouthpiece, put it to her lips, and buzzed. She had been practicing buzzing all weekend.

"Can I try that? Wow, is it heavy," said Ralph when Libby handed him the mouthpiece. He wiped it on his pant leg first before puffing up his cheeks and blowing. Only a rush of air came out.

"You're doing it all wrong. You have to *purse* your lips and then buzz 'em. Like this."

Libby decided too late that showing Ralph how to blow was a big mistake. Now she had to listen to him buzz his lips all the way to school.

Libby saw Ralph again at lunch. They sat in the fourth-grade section of the crowded gym that was used as a temporary lunchroom. "You want to go over to the park after school?" Ralph asked. "I figure we've got enough people for a soccer game."

"Okay," answered Libby, and then she remembered. "Shoot! I can't—I have tuba practice."

Ralph leaned toward her, cupping his hand over his ear. "You can't what?"

The gym was separated with a roll-away wall from the classes on the other side. Nobody liked it, especially the cafeteria monitors, who had to listen to the noise bounce off the wooden walls and high ceiling for two-and-a-half hours each day.

"I said," repeated Libby, only slower and louder this time, *"I have dumb ol' tuba practice."*

At three Libby went downstairs to the Dungeon. She wondered if Mr. Cheney would be standing on his head again or maybe doing something even weirder. Instead she found him in his office typing into a computer that sat on his desk. Libby quietly slid into her chair and, taking out the mouthpiece, connected it to the tuba. Then she placed her fingers over the first and third keys and buzzed.

Twenty minutes later Mr. Cheney, who hadn't said a word in all that time, called Libby over. "You're getting the hang of it," he said, looking up from the monitor. "But you need to count carefully. Make it steady; don't rush."

Libby glanced down at the writing on the monitor. The top right-hand corner was addressed to the *Post-Journal.* Her eyes followed partway down the screen and stopped abruptly: "HELP OUR STUDENTS FAIL."

The words jumped out at her.

Help our students fail? *Teachers aren't supposed to write things like that to the newspaper,* Libby thought as she wandered back to her chair. Soon she was having trouble buzzing her lips just right and holding the count longer. Even the boiler across the hall carried a steadier beat.

She imagined Mr. Cheney, hidden inside his office, gleefully rubbing his hands together while plotting Libby's failure. Could somebody actually fail band? Did getting kicked out of chorus count as failing? Okay, so Mr. Walinsky didn't exactly kick her out. But he made it pretty clear how he felt. With her luck, anything was possible.

After practice Libby hurried home. "Not tuna casserole again," she mumbled as she entered the kitchen through the back door. Noel was putting the casserole dish into the oven. "Why can't Mom make spaghetti more often?"

Noel closed the oven door with the back of her foot. "Honestly, Libby, I swear you could live on that stuff."

She shrugged. "So I like it." Libby started toward the door, then paused. "Noel," she said, turning back, "when you were at Lincoln, did you think Mr. Cheney was weird?"

"No weirder than you."

"Come on, I mean *really* weird. The other day when

I went for my lesson, Mr. Cheney was standing on his head."

Noel gave her an I-don't-believe-a-word-you're-saying look.

"Honest, I'm not faking you out. *It's true.* And then today during practice he was in his office writing something to the *Post-Journal.* All I saw was the first line, and it said, 'Help Our Students Fail.' Now that's *weird.*"

"Maybe he wrote that because he doesn't like kids who poke their noses into places they shouldn't."

"Some help you are!" Libby tramped off to her room.

By Thursday most everyone—thanks to Mike— heard about Libby taking up the tuba. "Picture Libby and the tuba," said Mike that morning when she walked into class.

"Yeah," agreed Charlotte. "Now she's got more than a music book to throw at the teacher." Everyone laughed.

At least the day wasn't a total loss. A substitute teacher came in for Mr. Cheney. Libby spent the whole hour working hard on the four assigned pages. But with all the blowing, she ended up with a headache.

By Friday, Libby hoped Mr. Cheney would still be

out. But no luck. He was waiting for her, right-side up this time, at exactly five after eleven in the Dungeon.

Libby quietly slid into her chair behind the tuba.

"You can start by warming up with the scale on page three," said Mr. Cheney, folding his arms.

Libby moistened her lips and buzzed. *VOOOOM.* Pressing more valves, she moved up and then down the B-flat scale, making two sour notes along the way. Where was the boiler-room monster when she needed it most to cover up her mistakes?

Mr. Cheney inched his chair closer. "Now, let's try that again."

With Mr. Cheney practically hovering over her, Libby started to wiggle uncomfortably in her seat. More sour notes came out. Grimacing, Libby waited for Mr. Cheney to say something about her awful playing. But he didn't. Instead he asked, "Getting dizzy?"

Libby nodded.

"It's important to breathe from the stomach," Mr. Cheney said. "And rest a bit after each exercise. Let's take a short break now."

After a minute he asked, "Are you ready?" When Libby nodded, he added, "Okay, let's go over that scale again. Only this time we'll try something a little different. Let's work on half notes."

Half notes? How could she make her fingers go any faster?

"One . . . two . . . ready . . . begin," counted Mr. Cheney.

Libby began pressing the keys. Just as she thought, her fingers were stumbling all over each other. She started the scale over. But with Mr. Cheney sitting so close and maybe waiting for an excuse to fail her, Libby's fingers suddenly froze. "I can't *do* it!" she cried. Scrunching down in her chair, Libby waited for Mr. Cheney to yell at her.

"I'm not going to bite your head off," he said. "It's okay if you don't get it right the first time or even the fifteenth." Mr. Cheney leaned back and looked directly at her. "If you think about it, Libby, the things in life that come hard, that really challenge us, we end up valuing the most. Like learning to play the tuba or working to make right what we believe is wrong."

Mr. Cheney smiled, and Libby noticed that his smile reached up to his dark brown eyes. "Now, try to relax and not worry so much. Okay?"

Taking a deep breath, Libby pressed her lips to the mouthpiece and buzzed. This time she played the B-flat scale with only one mistake.

• • •

That night after supper, while Libby was watching TV, Mr. Bloom came into the living room with a folded section of the *Post-Journal* in his hand. "Emily," he called to Mrs. Bloom, who was curled up on the couch, reading a magazine. "Have you seen tonight's Readers' Forum?" Before she could answer, he added, "Here's one written by a teacher at Lincoln."

Libby turned from the screen and looked up at her father.

"It's titled, 'Help Our Students Fail,'" said Mr. Bloom, and he began reading the article aloud. "'Beginning next September, the students of Lincoln School might have to put away their clarinets, flutes, drums, and horns. Why? Because the school board is currently considering a cost-saving proposal to eliminate the band program.'

"'The board has already tightened its financial belt by combining classrooms and eliminating such extracurricular activities as team sports. Now the belt might be inched a little tighter. Of course, squeezing off programs that enrich and empower students as individuals should not be part of the deciding factor.'

"'Cost-effectiveness must be first and foremost. After all, taking away music from our students' lives is a small price to pay compared to the money saved.'"

Libby scratched her head. "Mr. Cheney sure has a

funny way of saying something. I mean, with him being a music teacher and all."

"It's not what you think, Libby," began her mother. "Mr. Cheney is saying one thing, but he means something else. It's called irony, or tongue-in-cheek. He's really saying that by taking away something as important as music in our children's lives, we're in a way helping them fail."

"I don't get it," said Libby. "Why doesn't Mr. Cheney just come out and say that?"

Mr. Bloom laughed. "Maybe because he wants to get people's attention."

Libby recalled Mr. Cheney's words to her earlier that day. "The things in life that come hard, that really challenge us," he had told her, "we end up valuing the most. Like learning to play the tuba or working to make right what we believe is wrong." He wasn't only talking about her, Libby now realized, he was talking about himself too. "Daddy, can I have that?"

After her father handed the page to her, Libby went to the kitchen, where she cut out the article, and brought it upstairs to her room. Sitting on the edge of her bed, she read the piece over three times. There was more to Mr. Cheney than she first thought, Libby decided. And she was . . . What was the word Mr. Cheney himself had used? Intrigued.

4

Band or Bust

"LOOK WHAT MY UNCLE Dick bought me," said Ralph when Libby stopped at his house Saturday morning. He held up a metal whistle that hung on a chain around his neck and blew into it.

Libby covered her ears.

"I told Uncle Dick about next Friday. You know, how us kids are dressing up like our favorite teacher. And I'm going to be Coach Dunn. Anyway, Uncle Dick said he wanted me to have a special whistle." He blew it again.

"Oh, brother," murmured Libby. Until Ralph reminded her of it now, she had completely forgotten about Teacher Recognition Day.

Libby took a newspaper clipping out of her pocket

and unfolded it. "Did you see this in yesterday's *Post-Journal*?"

Ralph, glancing over his shoulder at her, wrinkled his brow. "Are you kidding? I don't read that stuff."

"I don't either, but my dad read it to my mom and me. Mr. Cheney wrote this about Lincoln." By the time Libby finished reading, Ralph had started up a game on his computer. Libby went over and sat beside him. "What do you think?"

"So Cheney wants the school to save a few bucks." Ralph handed her one of two joysticks.

"You don't understand. My mom says he doesn't really mean that at all. She had a funny name for it when somebody says one thing but means the opposite."

"Who cares? Come on, let's play the game."

"Well, for one thing, *I* care. What if I want to join band again next year? I might not get the chance because it'll already be decided for me and everybody else. I think Mr. Cheney is right."

"What else would he say? If they cut out band, he could lose his job next year."

"If anybody loses their job, it should be Mr. Walinsky."

Ralph made a face.

"So Cheney's strict about some things. But he's really okay."

"How come you've got Cheney on the brain all of a sudden?" Ralph glanced over at Libby. "Are you gonna play or not?"

"My dad said that if enough people think Mr. Cheney is right, then maybe the school board won't—"

"For Pete's sake, Lib, either shut up or play."

Before Ralph had a chance to glance back at the screen, Libby punched the button on her joystick, knocking one of Ralph's men out of action.

For the first time since she took up the tuba, Libby was actually looking forward to practice the following Monday. At exactly three she went downstairs to the Dungeon. It was empty.

All during practice Libby kept expecting Mr. Cheney to walk in. After a while she forgot about Mr. Cheney and the noisy boiler room and the long crack in the cement wall. Soon she was concentrating on the notes in her lesson book and pursing her lips just enough so the sounds would come out right.

"Caught you red-handed," barked a voice from behind.

Startled, Libby lurched forward, knocking over the

music stand. She untangled herself from the tuba and was reaching down to pick up the stand when she saw a pair of oxfords from the corner of her eye. She looked up.

Mr. Cheney was in a tan overcoat. "It's four-ten. Anybody caught past their one hour of practice," he began, frowning, "gets to stay an extra hour every week for the rest of the school year."

Libby's mouth fell open. Another whole hour after school? What did she do to deserve that? "I guess I forgot the time," she mumbled, her face turning red as she put away her music folder.

Mr. Cheney, disappearing into the office, soon returned with a briefcase. This time he was grinning. His thick mustache turned up at the ends. "Yup, a whole extra hour." He winked.

Now she knew he really didn't mean that at all. "Oh, I get it, sort of tongue-in-cheek. Like what you wrote in the *Post-Journal* the other day." Libby followed Mr. Cheney out of the room.

"Tongue-in-cheek, eh?" Mr. Cheney locked the door. "Looks like I can't pull your leg and get away with it." His hearty laughter filled the basement as he began to climb the staircase. "I'm surprised you read the article and understood my point."

"My dad saw it first," said Libby as she hurried to catch up with him. "I didn't understand until my mom told me what you meant. Then it made a lot of sense."

Mr. Cheney paused a moment before turning toward Libby. "Most kids your age wouldn't give it a second thought. But you did, Libby. That tells me something about the kind of person you are." Nodding, he added, "I'd say someone with insight and maturity." He smiled. "I like what I see."

Libby felt a wave of heat move up her neck. Nobody had ever told her that, not even her parents, who loved her no matter what stupid things she did. And especially not Noel. "What do you think is going to happen, Mr. Cheney?"

"Unfortunately, the school is having a budget crisis. But if enough people are convinced that we need to keep the band going and some of the other programs, then they won't get cut," he answered. "You know, Libby, I have a confession to make. Remember what I told you earlier about coming in an extra hour? I meant it, but not in the way I made it sound. The extra hour is for band practice Friday afternoons."

Libby swallowed hard. It was too soon—she wasn't ready.

"I know this seems awfully soon," said Mr. Cheney as

though reading Libby's thoughts. "But you've been making a lot of progress, and I really can use you in the holiday concert. Five and a half weeks should give you enough time to work on the new songs and be ready."

Outside, Mr. Cheney tucked the briefcase under his arm as he started for his car. "Can I count on you?"

How could Libby say no when Mr. Cheney was counting on her? Especially since nobody had ever counted on her before for anything important. "I'll be there."

"Great!" Mr. Cheney waved before climbing into a red Firebird.

On the way home Libby wondered how she was ever going to be ready for the holiday concert. She couldn't even play something as simple as "Row, Row, Row Your Boat" without making at least one mistake.

Libby remembered her first lesson when she found Mr. Cheney standing on his head. "Seeing the world from a different angle," he had told her, "gives one a whole new outlook on things." Maybe, Libby decided, a new outlook was exactly what she needed.

At home, she went to her room and shoved her bureau away from the wall. Libby got down on her hands and tried to kick up her feet. *How did Mr. Cheney make it look so easy?* she wondered. Finally she got her feet up over her head, but her arms started to wobble, so

she knew she couldn't hold on for long. Libby came down with a crash.

"What's all that racket?" called Mrs. Bloom. Instead of getting a whole new outlook, all Libby got for her effort was a headache and her mom getting after her for being too noisy.

5

A Political Cartoon

LIBBY WAS AT HER DESK drawing funny faces in her notebook while Charlotte Whippo was up front reading her boring report on the Crusades. Charlotte finished and Mrs. Petrush, clearing her throat, zeroed in on Libby, who quietly put down her pencil. "Just because some of you chose a written over an oral report doesn't mean that you aren't to give your full attention to the speaker."

She glanced at the clock then. "I see that it's almost time for lunch. This is taking far longer than I expected. Gus and Amanda, you'll have to wait until tomorrow for your presentations."

Amanda raised her hand. "Mrs. Petrush, why can't we eat here in the room? Then Gus and I will have time to do our reports while everybody finishes up their lunch." When Mrs. Petrush started to shake her head, Amanda added, "*Nobody* likes to eat in the gym, and this would be something fun to do."

"Can we eat here?" another voice asked.

"Some of you need to buy lunch," Mrs. Petrush replied. "Besides, this period is my only afternoon break."

Libby waved her hand. "I was wondering . . . when are we going to get our old cafeteria back?"

"I wish I knew the answer, but I don't," said Mrs. Petrush. "You understand that the school doesn't have enough rooms."

"Charlotte," began Libby, "isn't your mom on the school board?" She already knew the answer, but Libby wanted to put her on the spot. After all, it was Charlotte who made a big deal over the burp incident.

"She's the president," reminded Charlotte.

"Then maybe you can tell us what the board's going to do about getting our cafeteria back. And what about the other things, like no more language club or team sports?" Libby could feel her face heating up as she continued. "Next year we might not even have band."

"It's time to leave, Libby," interrupted Mrs. Petrush.

"Not time for a full-scale discussion on the conditions here at Lincoln."

"But it's true; everybody knows it."

Several of the other kids started talking at once. To get their attention, Mrs. Petrush flipped the light switch twice. "We're not going to lunch until this room is perfectly quiet." The noise quickly settled down.

As they were leaving, Charlotte announced to the whole room, "For your information, Libby Bloom, my mother *is* doing something."

"Like what?" asked Libby.

Silently Charlotte marched out the door and down the hall.

Later that day a thought began to chew at the edges of Libby's mind. The more Libby mulled it over, the more she liked the idea. This wasn't silly or stupid, but something even Noel would approve of. She would write her own letter to the Readers' Forum, just like Mr. Cheney had done.

When she got home, Libby gathered up a dictionary, notebook paper, and a pencil. Dumping them on the dining-room table, she set to work. But after twenty minutes all Libby had written were several sentence beginnings and "Dear Editor" at the top.

Libby sighed. Maybe this wasn't such a good idea after all.

"Is this *the* Libby Bloom . . . the one who claims that homework is teachers' revenge?" said her mother, appearing in the doorway. She went over to the closet to hang up her coat. "The very same one who needs to be reminded to crack open the books?"

"*Mom,* you don't have to make a big production. Besides, this isn't—"

"You're absolutely right," Mrs. Bloom interrupted, putting her arms around Libby and giving her a hug. She went into the kitchen as Noel was coming out.

"The real Libby Bloom was kidnapped and taken up into a Martian spaceship," said Noel, biting into a celery stick stuffed with cream cheese. "At least they replaced the original with something better."

"Better than the reject they replaced you with."

Noel stopped beside Libby. "You wouldn't know the original from the reject if it was sitting on your nose."

Libby decided to ignore that. "Noel," she said, "can you help me with this?"

Noel looked down at the paper. "What is it?"

"I'm trying to write a letter to the Readers' Forum. It's about how Lincoln School is running out of space and that lots of things are getting cut. Like team sports, and maybe even band." Libby slumped down into her chair and sighed. "I don't know how to start."

Noel nibbled on her celery stick while she thought it over. Finally she said, "Forget the letter. Do what you're always doing around here."

"Huh?"

"Draw a cartoon. I don't mean just *any* cartoon. Wait, I'll show you," said Noel, going into the living room. She soon returned with last night's newspaper opened up to the editorial page. "Like this," she said, waving what was left of her celery at the picture. "It's called a political cartoon."

Reading the caption, Libby scratched her head. "Did the president really say that?"

"Of course not. It's supposed to be exaggerated. That's how you get the point across."

"Oh, I think I get it now."

"Is this for some kind of homework assignment?"

Libby shook her head.

"Then why bother?"

"Because . . ." Libby paused to think over her answer. Why *did* she care what happened? she wondered, and thought of the tuba and the fact that learning to play it was something hard to do. "Because things like band and team sports are important too, just like math and science and social studies."

Noel shrugged and wandered out of the room. Just then two ideas popped into Libby's head. One had to do with a political cartoon. And the other with Teacher Recognition Day.

Teacher Recognition Day

"IF YOU DON'T GET OUT of the bathroom in exactly ten seconds, I'm going to personally make sure you suffer the most humiliating experience ever imagined!"

Shutting out Noel's voice, Libby leaned toward the mirror and adjusted the fake mustache she had found stored in the basement among some old Halloween costumes. Not bad, she decided before putting it in her pocket for safekeeping.

Ever since last Tuesday, when Libby made up her mind about Teacher Recognition Day, it didn't take long for her to figure out who she was going as. The hard part was finding the right clothes.

"*Libby!*"

"Why don't you use the downstairs bathroom?" she hollered back.

"You know perfectly well Daddy is using it."

Libby stood up straight. "I'll be out in a couple of minutes." Her dad's green polka-dot tie and the blue jacket she had borrowed from Ralph would have to do. She squirted mousse into her short brown hair and combed it all back.

"Mother!" shrieked Noel, stomping away. "It's twenty-five minutes to eight and Libby isn't out of the bathroom yet. She's going to make me late for school."

After one final sweep with the comb, Libby unlocked the door and stepped out.

Noel raced down the hall and practically shoved Libby into the wall. Then she slammed the door in her face.

Downstairs in the kitchen Libby's father was getting ready to leave for work. As Libby slouched into her chair, Mr. Bloom paused by the door and looked over at her. "Hmmm. Even for you, Libby, that attire is a bit strange for school. Isn't that my tie?"

"*Daddy,* I already told you and Mom about Teacher

Recognition Day and who I was going to be. Don't you remember?"

"Oh, that's right. Well, happy Teacher Recognition Day," he said, giving her a wink and her mother a peck on the cheek before going out the door.

Libby scooped up her cereal and drank her glass of orange juice in record time. She wanted to leave before Noel came to breakfast and started bugging her again. Carrying her dishes over to the sink, Libby asked, "Mom, is there an old pair of reading glasses around here I could use?"

"I think I know where there just might be one," she said, and returned a few minutes later.

"Thanks." Libby slid the glasses into her pocket.

On the way to school Libby met up with Ralph, who was dressed in gray sweats with a blue stripe down the legs. He unzipped his jacket to show off the sweatshirt with COACH inked in black letters across the front. Around Ralph's neck was the whistle.

"For a second there I almost thought you *were* Coach."

Ralph grinned. "I still can't believe you actually dressed up as Mr. Cheney. Where's your mustache?"

"Right here," said Libby, patting her left pocket. "I've got something else to show you." Unzipping her book bag, she took out her political cartoon and handed it to Ralph.

"Hey, that's our school. And there's what's-his-face," Ralph pointed out, laughing.

"It's *Ms.* Stretch McKinsy, I want you to know."

"Yeah. Well, what I want to know is, when is she going to take off that goofy-looking hat so I can see what she really looks like?"

"What do you mean, goofy looking? I like it."

"I can tell," he said, nodding at Libby's own floppy hat.

"Ralph Corbet, I'm not walking with you anymore," snapped Libby as she speeded up.

"Hey, Libby!" squealed Amanda when Libby walked into the classroom. Amanda was in a long skirt and matching tank top, the kind Ms. Humphries often wore. "Are you *really* Mr. Walinsky?"

Placing the reading glasses on the tip of her nose, Libby drew the mustache from her pocket and put it on her upper lip. "Guess again," she said.

"*Mr. Cheney!*" yelled three voices at the same time.

"Leave it to Libby to come up with the best *and* funniest," said Amanda.

Charlotte, dressed up like Mrs. Krauss, wore a mint-green suit with a red rose pinned to her lapel. "I think it looks stupid," she muttered.

That made Libby fume. "Hey, Charlotte, you never did tell us what your mother is doing about—"

"It so happens," interrupted Charlotte, her face matching the color of the red rose she was wearing, "she confided in me about that just yesterday."

Oh, sure, I'll just bet she did, thought Libby. "Well? What *is* she doing about it?"

Charlotte held her head high. "My mother is chairperson of the committee to study the problem. In fact, they've been meeting ever since last year."

"Studying it for a whole year? All the committee people have to do is come on down and see what's happening."

"That's right," agreed Mike.

"Don't any of you know that you can't just rush into something? Besides, my mother has a lot of other important meetings that keep her awfully busy." Then Charlotte whirled around and went over to her seat.

During study hall Libby thought over what Charlotte had said about the committee getting together since last year. And that gave her another idea. Taking a sheet of paper out of her notebook, she began to draw. By the end of the period, Libby had sketched a different political cartoon.

" This committee will continue studying the conditions at Lincoln School over the next hundred years. Meanwhile, all in favor of cutting out the band program raise your hands."

Libby was stepping into the Dungeon for band practice that afternoon when Mr. Cheney waved her over. "We've only been working on this for a couple of weeks, so you're not that far behind," he said, opening up the music folder on his stand. Mr. Cheney took the reading glasses from his jacket pocket and placed them halfway down his nose.

With a flourish, Libby took out her glasses and placed them halfway down her nose too.

"Hmmm," said Mr. Cheney, smoothing his mustache with the tip of his finger as he peered down at Libby. "Are you supposed to be someone I know?"

Nodding, Libby smoothed her fake mustache with the tip of her finger and looked up at Mr. Cheney.

"I'll be," he murmured, and grinned at her. "I'm flattered, Libby. I really am." His grin suddenly erupted into laughter and, for a moment, competed with the clanging noises coming from the boiler room.

But soon Mr. Cheney was back to business. "You'll notice I've made some changes here in your music. The difficult parts I've replaced with something easier, and accompaniments I've taken out altogether."

Libby took off her glasses to see better and stuffed the mustache back in her pocket. At least she wouldn't have to play the hard parts, but the music wasn't going to be a piece of cake.

Mr. Cheney closed the folder and handed it to her. "You'll do fine, Libby, I know you will. For now just concentrate on what you can play, and we'll go over the rest later at practice."

Libby crossed over to her chair in the center of the back row.

"Yo, Libby," called Mike, doing a roll on his drums. "That's some fancy outfit."

Mr. Cheney tapped his baton on the edge of the music stand. "Okay, ladies and gentlemen," he said, raising his arms, "let's warm up on scales." Everyone picked up their instruments. "Quarter notes, in concert B-flat. Ready and . . ."

At least she could do this without making too many mistakes. Libby was glad for the times she'd spent after school practicing boring scales.

"In eighth notes," called Mr. Cheney when they finished. "Same scale, only a light staccato this time."

After warming up on two other scales Mr. Cheney had them take "I Saw Three Ships" from their folders. Libby looked at the notes. Even with the changes, this piece was a lot harder than anything she'd ever played.

When the baton went up, Libby pressed her lips to the mouthpiece and readied her fingers over the keys.

"Keep it steady."

With her left foot curled around the chair leg, Libby tapped her right foot on the wooden floor.

"You're mushing it together . . . *Accent!*" shouted Mr. Cheney above the music.

How could she possibly accent when she couldn't get out all the right notes? If she were one of fifteen clarinet players, it wouldn't matter. Since she was the only tuba player, however, all her mistakes reverberated over everyone else. But she was grateful Mr. Cheney never once said anything that embarrassed her in front of everybody.

"Let's try that again."

"One, two, three," she counted without looking up. Libby blew. The sound of an A-flat echoed in the quiet of the room.

Everyone was staring at her. Of all times not to look at Mr. Cheney. She wasn't ever going to be ready for the holiday concert. Not this year's, anyway.

"Where do you live?" Mr. Cheney asked Libby after practice. When Libby told him, Mr. Cheney added, "That's not too much out of my way."

"If . . . if you want to talk with my mom and dad, I think you should know that they don't get home till *real* late."

"Perish the thought, Libby. I didn't ask for that reason. If it's all right with you, though, I'd like to drop off the tuba at your house. Then you can have the whole weekend to practice."

This was the kind of help she could do without. After all, it was bad enough she had to face the tuba at school almost every day. Of course, she didn't tell Mr. Cheney that. Instead she nodded and mumbled, "Thanks."

7

The Readers' Forum

WHEN SHE GOT HOME, the tuba was waiting by the front door. Libby set it up in the family room and began to play "I Saw Three Ships." Noel bounded into the room. "Honestly, Libby, can't you find a better place to practice before the whole family goes totally deaf?"

Libby cupped her hand over her ear. "Eh? What ya say?"

Whirling, Noel started for the kitchen. *"Mother,"* she called, "make Libby practice someplace else. Like in the basement."

Ignoring her, Libby turned back to her music folder and, pressing her lips to the mouthpiece again, buzzed. She still made a lot of sour notes. And sometimes it was even hard to tell what she was playing. But with each effort, Libby noticed, she played a tiny bit better.

When her mother called everyone to supper, Libby glanced at her watch. "A whole forty minutes?" Libby couldn't believe how fast the time had gone. And she wasn't even dizzy.

After supper Libby went to her room to work on her political cartoon. When she finished, her final drawing had a view of the board room in the first panel and the overcrowded school in the second.

Afterward Libby gathered up Friday's newspaper, along with an envelope and stamp she found in her father's desk, and spread them out on her bed. Inside the newspaper on the editorial page Libby found what she was looking for. The boxed-in information read: "All letters to the Readers' Forum must include the writer's signature, the correct full name and address of the author, and a telephone number for verification purposes."

Easy enough, Libby decided.

She read on: "The editor reserves the right to reject or edit all material."

Now *that* could be a problem. What if her political cartoon was rejected because it wasn't a letter? Maybe if she explained her reason for the drawing, it wouldn't get rejected. Libby got out a sheet of notebook paper and began to write the date, her address, and her telephone number in the top-right corner.

"*Dear Sir,*" she began, and paused.

Didn't Mrs. Petrush tell them last week in English class that they should try to find the proper person to address their letters to?

Libby started to look through the *Post-Journal* again. On page two she found the address and name of the editor. Erasing *Sir,* she continued writing:

Dear Katherine Myers,

My name is Libby Bloom, and I'm a fourth-grade student at Lincoln. I drew this political cartoon to show what is happening at my school. I hope you will publish my cartoon (even though it isn't a letter) in your Readers' Forum.

Thank you,
Libby Bloom

Afterward Libby quietly slipped the sealed envelope into their mailbox.

Every day over the next few weeks, Libby eagerly looked for her cartoon in the Readers' Forum. But every day turned out to be a disappointment.

The first Thursday in December, Libby sat in the Dungeon playing the tuba. She tried to push the cartoon out of her thoughts.

"Not so heavy on the accent," said Mr. Cheney. "Make it a little quicker and lighter, and it should work out better. Okay?" From the boiler room next door came a loud rumble. Mr. Cheney rolled his eyes. "How many bands can boast of having a noisy boiler as part of their percussion section? Unfortunately, it has a tin ear and can't hold a beat."

Libby smiled. When the boiler finally quieted down, she buzzed her lips, making sure the sounds came out quick and light.

Nodding his approval, Mr. Cheney did his Humphrey Bogart impersonation. "Stick with me, kid. You got what it takes to be a great tubist."

"Tubist?"

"Sure. There are clarinetists and flutists and violinists. Right? So," Mr. Cheney continued, shrugging, "why not tubists? I kind of like the word myself."

"But there are also trumpeters," Libby countered, "and drummers and . . ." She stopped when she realized that tuber was even sillier than tubist. Putting her hand over her mouth, she stifled a giggle.

"Well, we can always fall back on tuba player. Of

course, it doesn't have quite the same pizzazz," he continued, giving her a wink.

Libby couldn't help it; she laughed out loud. It was his corny sense of humor that usually got to her. But there was something more to Mr. Cheney—something that made him special—although she wasn't yet certain what it was.

That night Libby sat on the floor of the living room, helping her father take Christmas tree decorations from two large cardboard boxes. "Dad, you know the letters people send to the Readers' Forum? Well, does it take very long to get them printed in the newspaper?"

Earlier Libby had raced to the front porch when she heard the thud of the newspaper landing. Once again, it had been another letdown.

She started to untangle a string of Christmas lights while Mr. Bloom climbed up a stepladder to attach a ten-point star to the highest branch. "Why do you want to know?" he asked.

Libby shrugged. "Just wondering."

"I have no idea. I've never written a letter to the editor." He started to climb down. "Are those lights ready?"

Libby handed them to him.

Just then the phone rang. "I'll get it!" yelled Noel, pounding down the staircase. It sounded like a herd of stampeding elephants. She was always trying to get to the phone first in case some guy with the jerky name of Eugene was calling.

"Mom," called Noel, "it's for you."

Libby was helping her father with another set of lights when Mrs. Bloom rushed into the living room. "Has anyone seen tonight's *Post-Journal?*"

"I put it in the magazine r—"

Before Mr. Bloom could finish, Mrs. Bloom had pulled out the newspaper and was opening it up. "There it is!" Folding back the page, she pointed out Libby's drawing at the top.

How had she missed seeing it? Libby wondered, until she noticed "Readers' Forum continued" at the top of page seven. Below the headline was a box enclosing the words "Editor's note: Miss Libby Bloom is a fourth-grade student attending Lincoln School."

"That was Grandma Bloom," Libby's mother informed them. "She called to see if we had seen Libby's cartoon."

"Will you look at that," said Mr. Bloom, taking the paper. "So that's why you asked about the Readers' Forum, Libby," he said, laughing. Her mother was chuckling over it too.

Why were her own parents acting as if it was some kind of joke? This was serious. Didn't they know that? "In case you and Daddy didn't notice, I was trying to make a point."

"We certainly did notice," said Mrs. Bloom, smiling at Libby. "Your point comes through loud and clear. We were only laughing at the humor."

Mr. Bloom put his arm around Libby. "What we have here is a budding political cartoonist."

"Could be, Daddy." Libby turned a thought over in her head. "Or maybe a music teacher."

"Who's to say you can't be both?" He gave her a hug.

"Was that *really* your name in the newspaper yesterday?" Mike asked Libby the next morning at school.

Before Libby could open her mouth, Ralph answered, "The one and only."

"Awesome." Mike gave her a high five.

It turned out that Mike wasn't the only one to see the cartoon. Other kids mentioned it as they passed Libby in the hall.

"Great stuff, Libby!"

"Way to go!"

Libby was about to step inside the classroom when

she heard "Hold it right there!" Libby peered over her shoulder. Charging down the hallway, like General George Custer leading the battle at Little Bighorn, was Charlotte. She stopped abruptly beside Libby.

"Is something the matter?" asked Libby.

"*Is something the matter?*" Charlotte repeated, raising her voice. "You're not going to get away with making up lies about my mother! She's seeing her lawyer right now. We're going to sue you and your family for everything you've got." Whirling, she stomped into the classroom.

The cluster of kids nearby slowly melted away. Libby felt every eye on her as she shuffled inside and over to her chair. Could Mrs. Whippo really sue her and her family? For everything they'd got?

Taking the Bull by the Horns

LIBBY WAS GLAD when it was time to escape to the Dungeon. She was sliding into her chair behind the tuba when Mr. Cheney called, "Congratulations on your *Post-Journal* debut." Grinning, he gave Libby a thumbs-up.

Libby hid behind the music stand, pretending to be busy rearranging the sheet music in her folder. She started to think about band and how she probably wouldn't be in this mess right now if it wasn't for that burp and Charlotte Whippo. Of course, then she would have been stuck with Mr. Walinsky for a whole year. Not a pleasant thought, Libby decided.

During practice, Mr. Cheney repeated twice like a litany: "This is it, ladies and gentlemen. Our last chance to pull it all together before," and he paused before adding, "the big one." The big one meant the holiday concert next Tuesday.

Libby was finding it hard to concentrate on the music. The fact that one of her valves wouldn't cooperate didn't help matters. "Mr. Cheney," said Libby, raising her hand, "one of my valves is sticking."

Mr. Cheney came over to take a look. When he unscrewed the valve from the back, a spring popped out. "Stop in my office later and we'll put some oil on it." Handing the key and spring back to Libby, he added, "For now, use spit."

By the end of practice Libby, who had been thinking over Charlotte's words, completely forgot about the oil. She got up so fast she almost toppled over the tuba. Then she hurried out the door ahead of everyone.

That night during supper Libby quietly picked at her mashed potatoes and meat loaf. She hated meat loaf.

The phone rang. "I'll get it!" cried Noel, and was at the phone before the second ring. "Hello?" she said, her super-sweet voice melting into the receiver. A pause and then, "Oh . . . yes, she's here. I'll get her for you." There was a definite note of disappointment in her voice. "It's for you," she said, holding the receiver out toward Libby. Then to Mrs. Bloom, she said, "Can I leave now?"

Ralph knew not to call between six and six thirty, when they were having supper. Could it be Amanda or someone else from school? Libby took the phone. With one hand clamped over the mouthpiece, she turned to Noel and whispered, "Who is it?"

Shrugging, Noel started for the living room.

"Uh, hello?"

"Hello. Is this Libby Bloom speaking?"

"Uh-huh."

"This is Marietta Whippo."

"Who?" asked Libby, not quite believing what she had heard.

The voice repeated it, only slower this time. "Marietta Whippo . . . Charlotte's mother?"

Libby tried to concentrate on Mrs. Whippo's words, but her head was spinning from what she was hearing. "I do hope you and your parents will plan to come to the school board meeting Monday night," said Mrs. Whippo. "The meeting begins at seven o'clock."

Libby, not knowing what to say next, stammered out, "Thank you," before putting back the receiver.

"Well, it certainly was nice of Mrs. Whippo to

personally invite you to their meeting," said Mrs. Bloom after Libby repeated her phone conversation. Her mother smiled broadly across the table at Libby. "I can hardly believe the president of the school board would call you up. Your drawing must have made some impression."

"Mom, Daddy . . . this isn't what it looks like. She wants me there all right, but not for the reason you think." Taking a deep breath, Libby went on to tell them about Charlotte's accusation. And what she and Mrs. Whippo were planning to do.

"You did nothing wrong."

Mr. Bloom's words didn't reassure her.

"Look, Libby," he said, "I really think Mrs. Whippo wants you there to express your own feelings on the matter. That's all. She can't sue you or us for what you drew. Didn't she tell you the meeting was open to the public? The way it looks to me, the board wants to get different points of view."

Even if her father was right—and Libby still wasn't all that certain he was—what could she possibly say to a bunch of grown-ups that would make any difference? Even more important, did she want to go? Before she had a chance to make up her own mind, both of her parents were already planning on having supper early Monday so they could leave at six thirty sharp for the board meeting.

"I'm not going," said Libby.

"I'll make something beforehand, like a casserole dish, so one of you girls can pop it into the oven."

"*Mom*, you're not listening to me. I said I'm not going." Libby crossed her arms. "You and Daddy will just have to go without me."

"We were planning to go *because* of you. I'd think after putting all that time and thought into your drawing, the meeting would be important enough for you to attend. Of course, it's entirely up to you, Libby."

Libby looked down at her plate. The mashed-potato dam holding back a pool of gravy had broken, drowning her peas. This was turning out to be the worst day in her life, Libby decided. She even forgot to ask her mother to pick up the tuba at school so she could practice over the weekend. The way things were going, it wouldn't have done much good anyway.

Leaning her elbows on the table, Libby sighed.

"Sometimes you have to take the bull by the horns." Mr. Bloom was spooning gravy from the server onto his potato.

Libby wrinkled her brow. "What, Daddy?"

"That's an old saying. It means you have to take the

first step in facing a hard or difficult situation. Worrying over it won't solve anything."

That was exactly what she was doing now—worrying over it. And it wasn't solving a thing, only making her worry all the more. Libby sat up. Stabbing her fork into the meat loaf, she decided it was time to take the bull by the horns.

The Plan

"WHAT'S UP?" asked Ralph the next morning when Libby called.

"You've got to come over—pronto," Libby said. "It's real important." Then she hung up.

When he got to the Blooms' back door, Libby was waiting. She grabbed his arm. "We've only got this weekend to get everything done," she said.

"Huh? Get what done?"

"Come on."

On the way to her bedroom Libby told Ralph about Mrs. Whippo calling her up yesterday. "Can you believe she invited me to go to the committee meeting on Monday? But I've got a plan. A lot of kids, like you and me, don't like what's been happening at school, right? And it's not only us; it's cafeteria monitors and teachers like Mr. Cheney.

"What if—and this is the important part—a whole bunch of people showed up Monday night carrying posters that said things like, 'Keep Band in Our School' or 'Bring Back Team Sports'?"

A grin began to slowly spread across Ralph's face. "Oh, I get it."

"My parents are going. Do you think you can get yours to go too?"

"Piece of cake," answered Ralph. "But that's only six people."

"Not if we make sure there are a lot more than that," she said, getting up.

"Oh, yeah. Next you're going to tell me that we'll have to go out and grab people off the—"

"Hang on, I'll be right back." Libby soon returned with a telephone book. Picking up a pad and pencil from her bureau, she sat down beside Ralph and shoved the phone book into his hands. "I'll make a list of everybody we know at school and you look up their numbers." When they were done, Ralph took his half of the list home while Libby made her phone calls from the upstairs phone.

The first name on her list was Mr. Cheney. She had

never called up a teacher before and probably never would again. But Mr. Cheney was different. "Hello?" answered a woman's voice.

"Can I speak to Mr. Cheney?"

"May I ask who's calling?"

Libby replied, and a moment later Mr. Cheney was on the line. "What can I do for you?"

Libby told him about the meeting and asked if he could come. "We want to make sure enough people will be there to show support. My friend Ralph Corbet is helping me call up everybody we know from school. And we're going to make posters for people to carry."

"Are you two kids organizing this?"

"I guess you could say that."

"I was already planning on going, Libby. But now I'll be sure to be there with bells on my toes."

She pictured Mr. Cheney with dainty bells attached to his big toes. Libby giggled.

Amanda was second on the list. "I'll try real hard to be there," she told Libby. "But I don't know for sure because my mom might have to work that night."

"You've been on that phone a whole hour and a half," sputtered Noel when Libby hung up after the eleventh call. "Now it's my turn."

Libby clutched the receiver to her. "But this is for a very important cause."

"What cause?"

"Don't you remember the meeting at school on Monday night? I need a little more time. Please?"

Noel sighed. "Just make it fast." Before leaving, she added, "Was this your idea?"

"Uh-huh. Ralph and I are organizing the whole operation."

"This . . . from my geeky sister who can't even organize her own bedroom?"

"Come on, Noel, gimme a break."

Monday morning on the way to school Libby wondered if Charlotte had heard about the phone calls. Libby didn't have to wonder long. She was at her locker when Charlotte strode over.

"I know what you're really trying to do," she said, shaking her finger accusingly at Libby. "Calling everyone behind my back just so you can set them up against my mother and me."

"No, that wasn't what I was—"

"You probably think it's all a big joke!" Before Libby could say another word, Charlotte whirled and stomped off.

Libby never intended her political cartoon to hurt anyone. What if Mrs. Whippo misunderstood her intentions too?

That evening the auditorium was packed. Libby and Ralph, along with their parents, had arrived early so they could hand out the posters they had made.

As they were sitting down near the front Libby saw a tall, slender lady go up on the stage and sit at the head of a long rectangular table.

"Wow! Look at all the people," said Ralph, nudging Libby. She looked around the auditorium again to see if she could find Mr. Cheney. There he was, sitting on the opposite side near the wall.

"Mr. Cheney, Mr. Cheney!" called Libby, jumping up out of her seat and waving. He waved back.

Libby sat down just as the tall lady picked up a wooden gavel and tapped it on the table. It took a few minutes to get everyone's attention. After she introduced the other board members and herself, Mrs. Whippo called on the secretary to read the minutes of the last meeting.

"Before we open up this meeting for a discussion on various proposals for Lincoln School," began Mrs.

Whippo, "I would like to thank all of you for coming. I'm overwhelmed and pleased at your response. Also, I would like to personally thank Libby Bloom, a fourth grader attending Lincoln, for focusing our attention on the problem from a student's point of view. I believe she is here tonight."

Everyone started looking around and whispering among themselves. *Oh, no,* Libby thought in desperation. She was trying to slide down farther in her seat when Mrs. Whippo asked, "Would you please stand?"

Soon Libby was standing on two wobbly legs.

"There she is," called a voice from behind. A flash from a nearby camera went off, blinding Libby for a moment.

"Perhaps you saw her editorial cartoon in last Thursday's *Post-Journal,*" continued Mrs. Whippo, holding up a section of the newspaper with the drawing. "Libby's feelings come through not only with humor, but with sincerity. Her concern is that nothing is being done to correct the situation at Lincoln School. I want to assure her, as well as the other students here tonight," she said, looking around the room. "The board is doing all it can to find a suitable solution as quickly as possible."

After Libby gratefully collapsed back into her seat,

Mrs. Whippo's words gradually began to sink in. *Was that all?* she wondered. The way it sounded to her, nothing was settled.

Libby felt the disappointment clear down to her toes.

10

"The Big One"

THE NEXT DAY at school Charlotte acted as if nothing out of the ordinary had occurred, which, of course, was what Libby expected. It was only later, after supper, when the unexpected did happen.

They had eaten early because of the holiday concert. Libby was in her room, putting on a white blouse and blue skirt, when she heard Noel yell, *"Libby's on the front page of the* Post-Journal*!"*

Libby dashed for the staircase and almost collided with Noel, who was coming up.

"Honestly, Libby. Couldn't you think of something better than 'Keep Band in the School'? And did you have to make that horrible face at the camera?"

Libby grabbed the newspaper. In the photo she was

holding the poster in front of her. She was the only one standing and was closest to the camera. Printed below in bold letters was the headline: SCHOOL BOARD ASSURES COMMUNITY. Libby read on. "Residents and students packed Lincoln School auditorium last night for an open discussion on the school's economic problems. Board president Marietta Whippo told the crowd of about two hundred, 'The board is doing all it can to find a suitable solution as quickly as possible.' Support for the music program and for restoration of team sports came from several residents who attended last night's meeting . . ."

There it was in black and white. Nothing had changed.

On the way over to the concert, Libby felt her heart pump faster. *What if she came in on the wrong beat or her fingers stumbled over the valves?* she worried. Her cartoon and the phone calls and posters didn't make any difference. Then why should all her practicing either?

At school Mike called, "Yo, Libby, were you trying to break the camera last night?"

Everybody laughed except Mr. Cheney, who didn't say anything. He took her aside. "A little nervousness is good; it keeps you on your toes."

Libby sighed. "I guess so . . . Mr. Cheney," she

added, looking up at him. "Last night at the meeting . . . well, nothing happened."

"The first step is to get people interested. And involved. You know, Libby, most of those people might not have been at the meeting if it wasn't for your cartoon. Or the efforts of you and your friend Ralph."

"And your editorial," reminded Libby.

"You know what really counts? You tried. And gave it your best shot."

When it came time to perform, Libby took her place in the center of the second row. Two Christmas trees, brightly lit and decorated with spiraling chains and sequined ornaments, stood at opposing ends of the stage. Libby looked around. Her family and Ralph's sat together near the front.

As the auditorium slowly dimmed and the faces dissolved into blackness, Mr. Cheney walked out. Pausing a moment, he lifted the baton. "One, and, two, and . . ."

Libby buzzed her lips, keeping a steady beat with the tap, tap, tapping of her right foot. She played all the right notes and came in at the right places. But when Libby started the second verse of *Deck the Halls* a sour note came out. She blew again; out came another sour note.

Oh, no. Her third valve was sticking!

Libby unscrewed the valve and was taking it off when a spring popped out and disappeared. She got down on her knees and looked under her chair. When she didn't find the spring, she crawled to the next chair, and the one after that.

"Hey, you almost knocked my music stand over!" grumbled Mike. Other kids were complaining too, but Libby ignored them. That spring didn't disappear into outer space; it was on the stage somewhere and she was determined to find it.

Libby was crawling around the clarinet section when she noticed something shiny. Nestled in a tiny crack was her spring. Soon she was back at her seat, the valve put together and lubricated with the help of a little spit.

She had found the spring, but that didn't change the fact that she had messed up. Again. She should've stayed in chorus—this was much worse than a measly burp. Now she, Libby Bloom, had single-handedly wrecked the concert.

Libby glanced at the side exit. Leaving would be easy, but then she would be letting down Mr. Cheney and the band. Besides, there was one more song to play. How much worse could it get?

So when Mr. Cheney held up the baton for the

grand finale, she pressed her lips to the mouthpiece. She concentrated hard on each note, and came in at the right times.

At last, the concert was over. As applause thundered and the lights came on, she realized that she hadn't made a sour note or missed a beat in the whole song.

That was when Mr. Cheney gave her the thumbs-up sign.

She hadn't ruined the concert after all!

When the band and chorus were filing out, Ralph came up to Libby. He laughed after she explained what she was doing. "I can't believe you crawled all over the stage looking for that spring."

As they stood together in the jammed hallway straining to catch a glimpse of their families a stranger asked, "Didn't I see your picture in the *Post-Journal?*" Other people stopped to talk with her about it too.

"Hey, everybody," called Ralph when their families emerged from the crowd. "Libby is a big celebrity!"

"Well, I don't know about that . . ."

"And a great tuba player," he added, and poked her in the arm.

"*Tubist,*" she said, poking him back. "A great tubist."